JESUS ESCAPES FROM THE WICKED KING

The Holy Family were on their way to Egypt, leaving the wicked king far behind.

SAINT JOSEPH saddled the donkey, and Mary packed the things, and they started out in the middle of the night. Jesus, Mary, and Joseph got very tired on that long trip to Egypt. Two whole weeks they walked, all day long, in the hot sun and the wind and the dust. They did not grumble one bit. They were happy because they were doing just what God wanted.

IN EGYPT, Saint Joseph had to find a house. He had a hard time, and when he finally found one, it was a very poor place.

IT WAS hard for Blessed Mother and Saint Joseph to fix up such a poor old house and make it clean and homey. Mary missed her friendly neighbors, too. But she did the best she could, and was happy.

SAINT JOSEPH did not know the people in Egypt and had trouble finding a job. He was a carpenter, you know. Here he is, delivering a table he made. Saint Joseph was honest and good to people. He did the best he could even on little jobs, and he smiled at everyone. That is how he got more jobs to do. He made money enough to buy food and clothes for Jesus and Blessed Mother.

JESUS SMILED at all the neighbor children, and soon they came to play. He was good to everybody — the ragged children and the rich children.

AS LONG as old King Herod was alive, the Holy Family had to stay in Egypt. Really they did not *have* to, because Jesus was God's Son, and God could have made Herod die any minute — but He did not. He wanted to give him a chance to change his wicked ways. Maybe Herod would be sorry, and ask God to help him, before he got old and sick and died. But it was no use. The bad king died bad.

WHEN HEROD was buried and out of the way, God sent His big Angel to Saint Joseph again. He came one night when Saint Joseph was asleep. "Get up, Joseph, and take your Family home," the Angel said.

Saint Joseph called them, and Mary and Jesus got right up and began to pack.

IT WAS a long, tiresome trip back home. Now, God could have brought them all back home faster than a jet, if He had wanted to. But He did not. Why do you think the Holy Family did everything just like plain people do? God wanted them to show us how to act when we have to do hard things. God wants right-away obedience. Jesus and Mary and Joseph said, "We will do what God wants." And they did it right away.

NOW fold your hands, and close your eyes. Pretend you are walking along with Jesus and Mary and Joseph. Jesus is listening. Whisper to Him: "Jesus, I love being with You. I want to be like You. Please teach me how. Help me to remember You when I have to do hard things."

WHEN THE HIPPOPOTAMUS MET THE BIG RHINOCEROS

The Hippopotamus said: "How monotonous to have a horn! Don't people laugh about it?"

The Rhinoceros gave a snort, and this he did retort: "You're only jealous, 'cause you're born without it!"

how would you play If you had no games or toys or books?

When I was alone outside, without any toys, I used to play a game with myself that you could call "Staying In One Place." That was the main part of it: to stay in one place for a long time.

For instance, I would tell myself: now I am going six large steps to the left and there I will stay until the shadow of the lamp-post touches the front steps —or something like that. Sometimes I would walk as many as fifty paces. Or I would decide to stay next to the little lilac bush until Mrs. Snider came home from her walk with the baby.

But you see, that wasn't all. I wasn't only sitting there, I was also looking. The more you look, the more things you see. And when you sit or stand still in one place, you sometimes see many more things than you would if you were moving around.

For instance: have you ever seen a bird come so close that you could actually see the tongue inside its beak? Maybe you didn't even know that birds have tongues.

I have had ladybugs walking up and down my arms and butterflies sitting on my feet. Once a squirrel almost jumped into my lap, but—oh, was it scared when it found out I was alive!

Once I saw a battle between red ants and black ants. Another time I turned over a stone near the trash cans and found some strange bug-like creatures there. Later I found some more in a musty cellar. That made me think that probably they like it only where it is dark and cool. Where the trash cans are standing it is also shady and a little damp.

One day I saw a walking ball of cotton. But when I watched it long enough, I saw that it really was a little spider, carrying its giant-sized egg. I have also watched a spider make its web while I was playing my game. Then I remember seeing a snail walk up a post, leaving behind it a glittery, slimy trail wherever it went. I don't think I would know how dogs manage to walk with their four legs if I hadn't watched so many walk by in the street where I live while I was sitting on the curbstone, playing my game. It's an interesting game if you ask yourself questions about the things you see, and then try to find the answer.

LULLABY

The moon shines silver-bright—
Sleep you, my child.
The little birds now rest
With mother in their nest,
So may your sleep be blessed—
Sleep, sleep, my little baby.

The trees and flowers sleep,
Sleep you, my child.
Your mother watch will keep,
Sleep you, my child.

Your father will be gone
'Till all his work is done,
So sleep, my little one.
Sleep, sleep, my little baby.

Do not fear wind or rain—
Sleep you, my child.
The sun will rise again—
Sleep you, my child.
And in the morning's rays
Each creature chants its praise
To Him Who guides our ways.
Sleep, Sleep, my little baby.

Helpful Jack

"Where have you been, Jack?"
"In the field."
"Were you alone?"
"No."
"Who was with you?"
"Fred and Phil."
"What did Fred do?"
"He plowed."
"And Phil?"
"He watched Fred plowing."
"And what did you do?"
"I helped Phil watch Fred."

The Bear

"I have a bear."
"Show him."
"I can't."
"Why not?"
"He's holding me!"

The old woman

There was an old woman
Who lived under a hill,
And if she's not gone,
She lives there still.

CATECHISM AND OLD KALABI

Brother Bill was working hard on the little church on the hill. Each day the church grew bigger and bigger. It would soon be finished. All the people in Matongu were interested in the building. They had never seen such a big place before.

Brother Bill was building the church with big bricks that had been baked hard in fire. He wanted the church to last a long time and he knew how to build it well. It was to have a thatch roof just like the huts of the people in Matongu until he could find the right kind of clay for tiles.

Nearly everyone in Matongu was helping. Some of the men could carry as many as twenty-two bricks on their heads at one time, and even the children were helping. Sunny was one of the boys who carried little baskets of sand and gravel to the spot where the mortar was being made. Sunny watched all these goings-on carefully and he felt quite sure that he would be able to build the next building all by himself.

The Guardian Angels were as happy as the people of Matongu. It was not every day you could watch a house being built for God, and the Angels wanted to be very sure that everything turned out well.

The Angels knew that the devils were not at all happy about the new church. They knew that the devils would try to get everyone to make mistakes on the building. So, the Angels kept very busy trying to make sure that each person did his job right.

The people who were not helping came to watch the

building and they sat around in groups watching and talking. Whenever he could, Father Christopher talked to them, and with the help of the Guardian Angels, they learned lots of things, especially about God.

Sunny's mother Ntaka-Ntaka and her friend Mulaya sat talking about everything that was going on in the village, while Sunny and Ngomi helped Brother Bill.

"Aya!" said Mulaya in surprise one day. "Who ever heard of such a big hut. Father George's God must be a wonderful God if He has such a big house to live in. Surely He will bring good fortune to the village. We shall have lots of rain, and the bananas will grow bigger and bigger than ever before, and we shall have lots of banana beer."

Father Christopher happened by just then and heard the part about banana beer, so he decided to tell them a story. Like most people in the world, the people of Matongu love stories, and soon a crowd had gathered to listen to him.

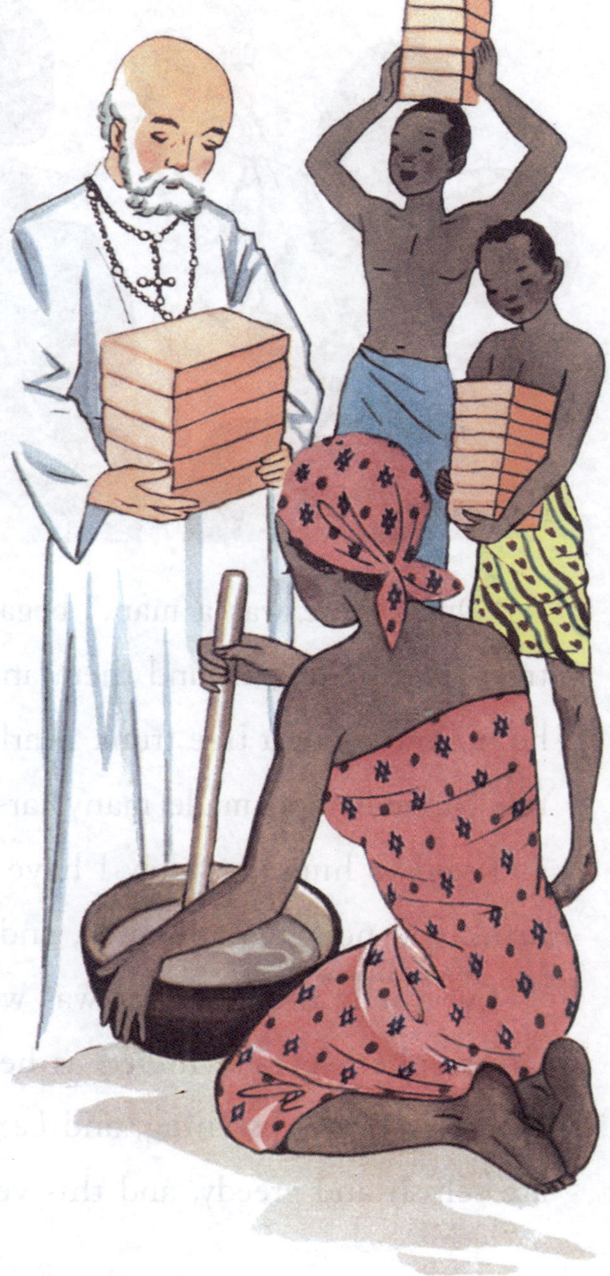

"Once there was a man," began Father Christopher, "who had some wonderful banana trees, and he dug around them and watered them and they grew lots of fine bananas. Then he hollowed out a tree trunk nearly as big as his hut. He filled it with bananas, and squeezed the bananas, and made many jars of fine banana beer. Then he sat down outside his hut and said to himself, "Now I have much banana beer. Tomorrow I will drink and drink and drink and not give any away, and I shall be happy and dance and sing."

Everybody thought that was wonderful and wished they could be that man. But Father Christopher's eyes twinkled as he went on: "But someone heard him," he continued, "for *Leza* (God) was listening, and *Leza* said: 'Foolish man, you have your banana beer, but you are selfish and greedy, and this very night you must make an account of your life.'"

"While the man was sleeping and dreaming about the beer, *Leza* came and took his life, and so the man died. Because he was selfish and greedy, he went to the place where bad men go. In the morning the neighbors came and found him dead, so they buried him, and then they drank all his banana beer at the funeral, and they were very happy. So," said Father Christopher as he finished his story, "if you want to be happy, try to please *Leza* while you are alive, for *Leza* is good and wants you to be good. If you are bad He will surely punish you."

"Father," said Ngondanie, who was Mulaya's husband, "tell us more about *Leza*."

"Ah," said Father Christopher, "if you want to hear more you will have to come to catechism class, for there is much to tell." And he gave them each a medal to wear around their necks, and they all said they would like to come.

Everything was going along fine, which made the devils very unhappy. They started mixing things up right away and doing all they could to keep everyone from learning about God's love. This is what happened the evening before catechism class, as the people sat around talking:

"Aya," began Mulaya, "but Father Christopher is a wonderful man. He knows all about *Leza* and he will teach us."

"Ha!" said Kalabi, who was sitting there smoking a long pipe with six bowls all full of tobacco, "are you foolish! Why, you'll just learn about the God of those priests, and the spirits will be angry! The spirits of the trees will be angry, and you will have no bananas at all; the spirits of the water will be angry, and you will have no rain; the spirits of the mani will be angry, and you will all die. Then Father George and Father Christopher will laugh and laugh and say that you are foolish like children."

There was a moment of silence after this, and even Mulaya and Ntaka-Ntaka looked frightened. Wupsy and the other Guardian Angels were watching, and then Ntaka-Ntaka's Guardian Angel whispered in her ear. Ntaka-Ntaka listened, and then she said: "Kalabi, when you were as small as my little boy, you were a bad boy, and now that you are as old as the big trees of the forest, you are a bad man. We would be foolish if we listened to you. Father George and Father Christopher and Brother Bill are good men. When my boy was burned, it was Father George who made him better. When my boy and Ngomi took the pink pills, it was Father George who made them well again. Even you, Kalabi, when you have a pain in your insides that jumps, you also go to Father George for help! No," said Ntaka-Ntaka finally, "you are a bad man, and the Fathers are good men. Your words are bad words, but the words of Father Christopher are good words, and I shall go to catechism class and learn all about *Leza*, and I shall be happy. But you, Kalabi, with your spirits and your mani, you will be unhappy. No, I shall not listen to you."

These were not only the words of Ntaka-Ntaka, but of Wupsy and the other Guardian Angels too. Everybody listened, and everybody agreed that Kalabi was a bad man and that he'd better not say any more bad things about the good Fathers, and if he did, he had better watch out.

Kalabi was very cross at this, but he didn't like the idea of the crowd being against him, so he kept silent.

The next day a big crowd went to catechism class, while Kalabi sat outside his hut and smoked his pipe and grunted.